FIDO

by Stephanie Calmenson

pictures by Maxie Chambliss

What a pup!

SCHOLASTIC INC.

New York   Toronto   London   Auckland   Sydney

ISBN 0-590-40410-5

Text copyright © 1987 by Stephanie Calmenson.
Illustration copyright © 1987 by Maxie Chambliss.
All rights reserved. Published by Scholastic Inc.
HELLO READER is a trademark of Scholastic Inc.
Art direction by Diana Hrisinko. Text design by Emmeline Hsi.

12 11 10 9 8 7 6 5 4 3 2 1   7 8 9/8 0 1 2/9

Printed in the U.S.A.   09

First Scholastic printing, November 1987

To Jaime and Erica Stechel.
                              —S.C.

To Deborah, the flying Basenji.
                              —M.C.

MR. Tinker was the head of a large
company that made and sold things.
He worked hard and sometimes
stayed at the office
until late at night.
The workers liked Mr. Tinker.
They thought he could do no wrong.

When Mr. Tinker went home
he was greeted by his loyal dog, Fido.

One day when Mr. Tinker's
alarm clock went off,
Mr. Tinker did not jump up as usual.
He did not feel well.
"Fido, I cannot go to work today,"
said Mr. Tinker.
"And there is an important
meeting this morning.
If only you could go in my place."

Fido stood up and wagged his tail.
"Well, why not?" said Mr. Tinker.
"You're a smart dog."

Mr. Tinker dressed Fido in his best suit

and fed him a hearty breakfast.

Then he gave Fido a box of
dog biscuits for lunch and
told him how to get to the office.

Take the bus at
the corner.

As soon as Fido left, Mr. Tinker
went back to bed.

Fido had no trouble getting to work.

He found his way to Mr. Tinker's office...

and sat down in Mr. Tinker's chair.

"Good morning, sir," said Norman,
Mr. Tinker's assistant.

"Woof!" said Fido.

"Bad cold you have there, Mr. Tinker.
I'll get you some tea,"
said Norman.

Fido liked the tea.

The phone rang.
Fido didn't like the noise.
"Grrr!" he said.

"I'll get that," said Norman.
"You should save your voice today."

Norman listened, then said,
"Ms. Potter wants to know where
the meeting will be, sir."

"Woof! Woof!" said Fido.

"Room two," said Norman into the phone.

At half-past nine,
Fido had to go out
for his morning walk.
Norman went with him.

They went across the street
to the park.

Fido ducked behind a bush.

"Nice day for picking flowers,"
said Norman.

Fido saw a cat and went after it.

"It's kind of you to try
to help that cat, sir,
but shouldn't we call
the Animal Rescue Squad?"
asked Norman.

"It's almost time for the meeting,
Mr. Tinker!" Norman called.
Fido ran back to the office.

The workers were ready
for the meeting.
"Woof!" said Fido,
bringing the meeting to order.

Everyone got to work.
They were trying to think of
something new to make and sell.
What Fido needed was flea powder.

"Itchy suit, sir?" whispered Norman.

"What about spinach lollipops?" asked a worker.

"Grrr," said Fido. He was hungry.

"You're right, sir," said the worker. "That wasn't a very good idea."

Fido took out his box of dog biscuits.

"Dog biscuits?" someone asked.
"You think we should make dog biscuits?"

"That's a fine idea!" said Norman.

Everyone agreed.
After all, it was Mr. Tinker's idea,
and Mr. Tinker could do no wrong.

Everyone was getting a pat
on the back.
Fido waited for his pat, too.

When he didn't get one,
he tried all his best tricks.

That night, Mr. Tinker greeted Fido at the
door and gave him an extra-good dinner.
"Thank you, Fido," he said.
"I feel much better."

The next day, Norman was glad to see
Mr. Tinker looking like his old self.
"We've started work on the dog biscuits.
That was one of your best ideas!"
Norman said.

"Why, yes, I guess it was,"
said Mr. Tinker.

They went into Mr. Tinker's office.
"We'll need a picture
of a dog for the box.
Don't you have a dog, sir?"
asked Norman.

Soon Fido's Tasty Treats
were in all the stores.
They were the best-selling
dog biscuits on the market.
Mr. Tinker was very proud of Fido.

People still stared at Mr. Tinker and Fido.
But instead of saying,
"That dog looks just like
his master," now they said,
"That man looks just like his dog!"

That made Mr. Tinker very happy.
He walked home with his head held high.